STORYTIME COLLECTION

This book belongs to

_____

_____

Autumn
Publishing

Published in 2018
by Autumn Publishing
Cottage Farm
Sywell
NN6 0BJ
www.igloobooks.com

LEO002 0518
2 4 6 8 10 9 7 5 3 1
ISBN 978-1-78670-758-1

Printed and manufactured in China

THE LITTLE MERMAID

Disney

STORYTIME COLLECTION

STORYTIME COLLECTION · STORYTIME COLLECTION

Long ago, deep under the ocean, the merfolk hurried to King Triton's palace. Today was the musical debut of Ariel, the youngest of his seven daughters.

Soon, everyone was packed into the palace.
However, the young princess was nowhere to be seen.

Instead of performing
at the palace, Ariel was busily
exploring a sunken ship. She loved to
collect treasures from the human world
and in her excitement completely forgot
she was due to sing at the palace.

As she swam about, something shiny caught
her eye. "Have you ever seen anything so
wonderful in your entire life?" she asked
her friend, Flounder.

From out of nowhere, a shark suddenly attacked them!
Ariel and Flounder swam as fast as they could through
the ship, dodging the snarling, snapping jaws. Luckily, the
huge, angry shark got stuck in the loop of an old anchor
and Ariel and Flounder managed to escape.

Ariel swam to the surface where Scuttle, a seagull who claimed to know all about the human world, was waiting for them. She excitedly showed him what she had found. "This is very unusual," he told her. "It's a dinglehopper. Humans use these to straighten their hair."

Suddenly, Ariel remembered she was supposed to be at the concert. "I gotta go!" she cried, as she swam quickly for home.

Unknown to the princess, she was being watched by Ursula, the evil sea witch who wanted to rule the undersea kingdom. "She may be the key to King Triton's undoing," said Ursula, as she watched Ariel through her crystal ball.

When Ariel got home, she explained to King Triton where she had been. "You could have been seen by one of those barbarians," he told her, before ordering her to stay away from the humans once and for all.

Upset by her father, Ariel went to the secret hideaway where she kept her collection of treasures from the human world. She soon started to feel better. "I wanna be where the people are," she told Flounder.

Despite her father's wishes, Ariel was soon swimming to the surface again. There, she saw a ship with fireworks exploding in the air all around it. Curious to see more, Ariel decided to get closer and was quickly joined by Scuttle. As she looked onto the deck, she saw there was a birthday celebration for a man called Prince Eric. "I've never seen a human this close before," said Ariel. "He's very handsome."

However, they were soon surrounded by a fierce
storm and lightning struck the deck, setting it
on fire. As flames engulfed the ship, the crew
lost control and crashed into some jagged
rocks. The impact knocked Eric off the
side and he fell into the ocean.

Ariel, who had seen the Prince fall, quickly dived
under the crashing waves and, with all her strength,
pulled him safely up to the surface and onto a beach.

"Is he dead?" Ariel asked Scuttle.

"I can't make out a heartbeat," replied the seagull, who was listening to Eric's foot.

"No, look, he's breathing," said Ariel, happily.

As Ariel sang to him, Prince Eric opened his eyes and gazed, half-dazed, at her face. Then, a dog bark startled the princess, who quickly dived back into the ocean, but Eric couldn't forget her beautiful voice.

Knowing his friend Sebastian had been keeping an eye
on Ariel, King Triton summoned him to ask how she
was. "Have you noticed she's been acting peculiar?"
asked the king.

Feeling nervous, Sebastian blurted out that she was
in love with a human. King Triton was furious!

The king confronted Ariel at her grotto. "I set certain rules and I expect those rules to be obeyed!" he cried.

"Daddy, I love him," she confessed.

King Triton couldn't believe it. "He's human! You're a mermaid!"

"I don't care," replied Ariel, who knew her love for the prince was real.

King Triton's trident began to glow as his anger grew. He was determined to keep Ariel away from the humans and believed the only way to do it was to destroy all her human treasures. "No," cried Ariel, "stop!"

Upset and alone, Ariel lay on the seabed, crying. Suddenly, two eels, Flotsam and Jetsam, approached her. "Poor, sweet child," they said.

"Who are you?" asked a frightened Ariel.

"We represent someone who can help you," they said, soothingly. "Someone who can make all your dreams come true. Just imagine you and your prince, together, forever."

With her heart aching to be with Prince Eric once more, Ariel was taken to see Ursula. "The only way to get what you want is to become human," said the witch.

"Can you do that?" asked Ariel, curiously.

"Here's the deal," said Ursula, who explained she could turn the princess into a human for three days. If Eric kissed her during that time, Ariel would be allowed to remain human forever.

I hereby grant unto URSULA, the Witch of the Sea one voice, in exchange for byon once high, Dinu eqihn thon birco serr'n Phur-gurr I re ht rasn retn t in scine urpl m srerp monk gux k, Ch ich noy ri imn io mund

for all eternity.
signed,

The offer sounded too good to be true, and it was. "If he doesn't kiss you," said Ursula, "then you belong to me!" There was also the matter of payment. "What I want from you is your voice," added Ursula.

Ariel was unsure but, afraid she'd never see Prince Eric again if she refused, reluctantly accepted. Suddenly, a green mist took away Ariel's voice, and Ursula locked it in a golden shell necklace.

The next thing she knew, Ariel was on the surface. She had legs, feet, even toes! She couldn't believe it and felt so happy. Sebastian, Flounder and Scuttle all agreed to help Ariel find her prince, though Sebastian was unsure they'd done the right thing. "What a soft shell I'm turning out to be," he grumbled.

Meanwhile, Eric had been visiting the beach every day in the hope of meeting his rescuer. Then his dog, Max, suddenly started barking and led his owner straight to Ariel. However, the princess couldn't speak to tell Eric she was the one he'd been searching for.

Believing Ariel was a shipwreck survivor, Eric took her back to
the castle. At dinner, Ariel charmed the prince with her behaviour,
especially when she started combing her hair with a fork!
"Very amusing," said Eric's guardian, Grimsby, who also found
the princess enchanting.

The next day, Eric took Ariel on a tour of the kingdom, ending with a boat ride on the lagoon. With Sebastian helping set the mood with some romantic music, the prince and princess slowly leaned in closer to one another. But, just as Prince Eric was about to kiss the girl, Flotsam and Jetsam overturned the boat.

Looking through her crystal ball, Ursula said, "At this rate, he'll be kissing her by sunset for sure." So, to make certain Ariel's soul would be hers, the sea witch decided to take matters into her own tentacles. Suddenly, she transformed herself into a beautiful young woman, who not only looked similar to Ariel, but had her voice, too!

That evening, as Eric gazed out to sea, Ursula began to sing just as Ariel had that day on the beach. The sound of her voice trapped the prince in a spell, making him fall madly in love with her.

The following morning, Ariel was shocked to discover that
Prince Eric was due to be married that very night. She was
devastated. "The wedding ship departs at sunset," said Eric,
who was hopelessly under Ursula's control.

As Scuttle flew alongside the wedding ship, he glanced into the porthole and saw the prince's bride looking into a mirror. He was shocked to see the reflection was Ursula.

Faster than he'd ever flown before, he headed back to tell Ariel. "The prince is marrying the sea witch in disguise!" he declared.

"What are we going to do?" asked Flounder, who knew Ariel's time was running out.

Ariel and her friends chased after the prince and Ursula. Scuttle, in a bid to stall the wedding and give Ariel time to reach the ship, gathered an army of animals, while Sebastian hurried to find King Triton.

Just as the couple were saying their vows, the animals
attacked Ursula. During the fight, the sea witch's golden
shell necklace broke, returning Ariel's voice to her and
releasing Eric from Ursula's spell.

"Eric," said Ariel, happily.

"You can talk?" asked Eric, who finally realised Ariel was the one who saved his life. "It was you all the time."

However, just as they were about to kiss, the sun set and the third day was at an end. "You're too late!" cackled Ursula, who transformed back into her original, hideous form. Ariel had become a mermaid again and her soul belonged to the sea witch.

"So long," said Ursula to the prince, as she dragged Ariel
into the ocean. As the witch pulled her deeper, King Triton
appeared. He tried to destroy the contract, but it was no
use. However, Ursula agreed that she would release the
princess, if the king took her place. Unable to see
her daughter suffer, King Triton agreed.

"At last, it's mine," laughed Ursula, who put the crown on her head and used the trident to grow so large that she towered over the sea's surface. As Eric jumped in the water to try and rescue Ariel, the sea witch stared down at them. "You pitiful, insignificant fools!" cried Ursula, as she started to create huge waves of water that threw Eric and Ariel apart.

The waves were so fierce, they dragged an old shipwreck up to the surface. Eric climbed on board. Fighting against the wind, the prince managed to steer the ship towards Ursula and, with the broken bow of the ship, pierced the witch's heart.

With everything back to normal, King Triton was finally able to see how much his daughter loved Prince Eric. Though he knew he'd miss her terribly, the king decided to turn her fins back into legs once more, so she could live on land with her prince.

Soon, it was Ariel and Prince Eric's wedding day. The ceremony was full of joy and laughter, attended not only by humans, but all the merfolk, too. When the pair finally kissed, everybody cheered. Together on land, they would live happily ever after.

THE END

COLLECT THEM ALL!

With 8 more exciting titles to choose from, you'll want to complete your Storytime Collection!

How far will a father go for his son?

Will Rapunzel learn who she truly is?

Will Moana be able to save the ocean?

Can Anna and Elsa stop an eternal winter?

Will Simba ever become king?

Will the Incredibles save the day?

Will Belle be able to break the curse?

Will Mowgli defeat Shere Khan?

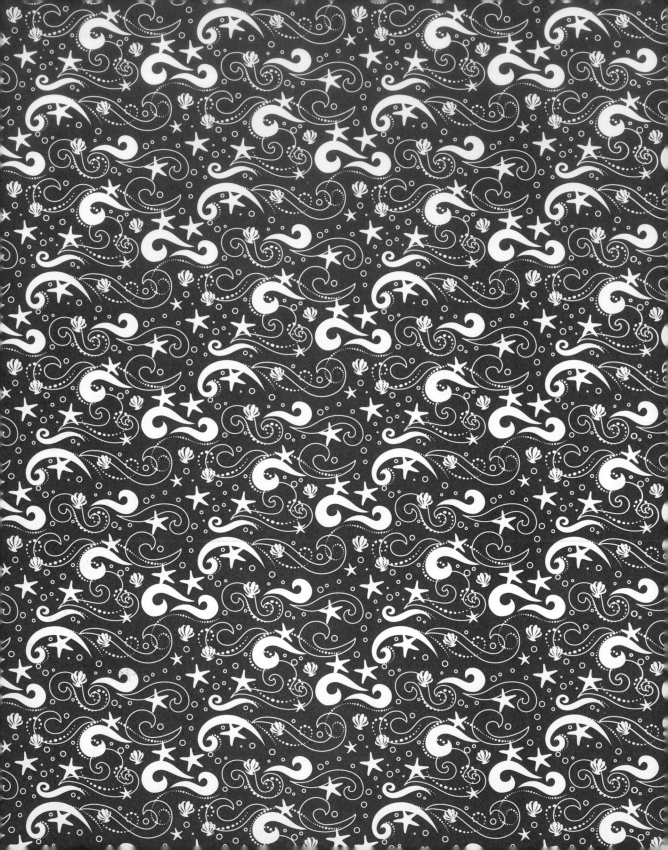